by Sam Watkins and
Louise Forshaw

Essex County Council

3013021577368 9

Franklin Watts

First published in Great Britain in 2016 by
The Watts Publishing Group

Text © Sam Watkins 2016
Illustrations © Louise Forshaw 2016

Series Editor: Jackie Hamley
Series Advisor: Catherine Glavina
Series Designer: Peter Scoulding

A CIP catalogue record for this book is available
from the British Library.

ISBN 978 1 4451 4594 5 (hbk)
ISBN 978 1 4451 4587 7 (pbk)
ISBN 978 1 4451 4593 8 (library ebook)

Printed in China

FSC
www.fsc.org
MIX
Paper from
responsible sources
FSC® C104740

Franklin Watts
An imprint of
Hachette Children's Group
Part of The Watts Publishing Group
Carmelite House
50 Victoria Embankment
London EC4Y 0DZ

An Hachette UK company.
www.hachette.co.uk

www.franklinwatts.co.uk

"I'm bored," said Tom.

Dad looked up from his newspaper. "Why don't you play outside?" he said.

"It's raining," said Liza.
"Splish, splosh," said Ollie,
their little brother.

"I know, let's do some painting," said Liza.

Tom got the painting stuff.

"Don't get in a mess," said Dad and went back to his paper.

paints

9

Liza painted a dinosaur.

Tom painted a castle.

Ollie painted his hands green.

"Ollie!" whispered Liza.
"Dad said, 'don't get in
a mess!'"

Tom painted an elephant.

Liza painted a giraffe.

Ollie painted his face green. "Raaah," said Ollie. "I'm a monster!"

Liza giggled. Ollie looked so funny!

Liza painted her face white. "Wooooo! I'm a ghost," she said.

18

Tom painted his face
yellow with black stripes.

"Grrrrr! I'm a tiger," he said.

Dad looked over his paper. "I thought I said *not* to get in a mess!"

23

The ghost and the tiger looked at each other.

"Raaah," said the monster.

Dad shook his head.
"I think it's time to play
outside now!" he said.

"But Dad, it's still raining," said Tom.

"Exactly!" said Dad.

Puzzle 1

Put these pictures in the correct order.
Now tell the story in your own words.
Can you think of a different ending?

Answers

Puzzle 1

The correct order is:

1b, 2d, 3e, 4a, 5c, 6f

Puzzle 2

Tom   The correct words are bored, fed up.

              The incorrect word is scared.

Dad   The correct words are shocked, surprised.

              The incorrect word is jolly.

Look out for more stories:

Bill's Silly Hat
ISBN 978 1 4451 1617 4

Little Joe's Boat Race
ISBN 978 0 7496 9467 8

Little Joe's Horse Race
ISBN 978 1 4451 1619 8

Felix, Puss in Boots
ISBN 978 1 4451 1621 1

Cheeky Monkey's Big Race
ISBN 978 1 4451 1618 1

The Animals' Football Cup
ISBN 978 0 7496 9477 7

The Animals' Football Camp
ISBN 978 1 4451 1616 7

The Animals' Football Final
ISBN 978 1 4451 3879 4

That Noise!
ISBN 978 0 7496 9479 1

The Frog Prince and the Kitten
ISBN 978 1 4451 1620 4

Gerald's Busy Day
ISBN 978 1 4451 3939 5

Dani's Dinosaur
ISBN 978 1 4451 3945 6

The Cowboy Kid
ISBN 978 1 4451 3949 4

Robbie's Robot
ISBN 978 1 4451 3953 1

The Green Machines
ISBN 978 1 4451 3957 9

For details of all our titles go to: www.franklinwatts.co.uk

bored   fed up

scared

shocked   jolly

surprised

Choose the words which best describe Tom and which best describe his dad in the pictures. Can you think of any more?